A LAKE TO REMEMBER

HOLDING ECHOES OF THINGS NEVER SAID.

SRINIVASAN NAIDU

For all those who saw something in me, even when I
didn't.

Your belief lit the path when I couldn't see the way.

This book exists because you did.

Contents

Preface — *vii*

Acknowledgements — *ix*

Author's Note — *xi*

1. The Plan — 1

2. The Road Unwinds — 8

3. Into The Stillness — 15

4. The Encounter — 21

5. The Disappearance — 25

6. A Promise Unkept — 30

7. Echoes In The Hills — 34

8. The Unsent Letter — 39

9. The Things We Carry Home — 43

Preface

Some stories come from imagination.

Some, from memory.

And a few, from that space in between, where the heart stores moments it never quite lived but somehow always felt.

A lake to remember was never planned. It began as a spark during a quiet evening, thinking back to a road trip I once took with my closest friends to Deoria Taal, a place so still, so beautiful, it felt like time had paused. We laughed, trekked, stared at the stars, and tried to freeze those fleeting moments in photographs and stories. But somewhere in the silence of those hills, a story waited to be told. Not ours exactly, but something deeper... stranger... and more haunting.

This book is born from that space.

It weaves together friendship, mystery, love, and loss, through a fictional tale, yes, but rooted in very real emotions. It asks: *What if the people we meet are more than they seem? What if some souls linger not to haunt, but to remember?*

As you journey with these four friends to the lake and meet Aanya, the girl by the fire, you may begin to feel that not everything here is fiction. Some echoes, I believe, belong to all of us.

Thank you for stepping into this story with me.

Acknowledgements

Writing this book has been more than just a creative journey, it's been a deeply personal one. I owe my deepest gratitude to everyone who stood by me with faith, encouragement, and patience, even on the days I doubted myself.

To my family and close friends — thank you for believing in me long before this story had a title or a single word on paper. Your support kept me going when the blank pages felt too heavy.

To those who read my poetry, followed @Awaara_insaan and @The_Impassioned_Writer, and shared their love for words, your quiet presence gave me the confidence to keep writing.

A heartfelt thank you to Falguni Solanki for your thoughtful help with the edits, your insights and care made this story stronger.

This story is fictional, but the emotions behind it are very real. It carries pieces of memories, whispers of friendships, and shadows of love, all shaped by the people who've touched my life in small but unforgettable ways.

Lastly, thank you to the readers, present and future, who chose to spend time with this story. I hope it stays with you, just like the girl by the lake stayed with us.

Author's Note

I didn't set out to write a book. I set out to capture a feeling, something that had been sitting quietly inside me for years: the ache of memories, the silence of things left unsaid, and the strange way certain places hold onto.

A Lake to Remember is a story born from longing, from the kind of friendships that shape us, from the love that doesn't quite leave, and from those fleeting moments in nature where time seems to pause and let us breathe again. It's about four friends, one trip, and a girl by a lake who wasn't supposed to be there... but somehow changed everything.

Writing this has been terrifying and beautiful. There were days I doubted myself, days I thought no one would care about this story, and nights where I stared at a blank page wondering why I was even trying. But I kept going, because this story meant something to me. And now, I hope it means something to you too.

If you're holding this book, thank you. Thank you for giving these pages a chance. I hope you find a little of yourself somewhere between the lines. Maybe in the laughter of the friends, maybe in the stillness of the lake, or maybe in the quiet heartbreak of things that never quite became.

This is not just a book, it's a piece of my heart I'm releasing into the world. I hope this story reaches far. But even if it touches just one person deeply... that's more than enough.

With all my heart,
[SRINIVASAN NAIDU]
Author of A Lake to Remember

1
The Plan

"Every great journey begins long before the first step — it begins with a longing."

1.1 — The Group Chat

The college WhatsApp group had been dead for weeks. Maybe even months.

Occasional "Happy Birthday!" messages surfaced like ghosts from another time — polite, automatic, quickly buried by silence again. Once a space of wild inside jokes, last-minute submissions, and 2 a.m. rants, it now felt more like a waiting room for nostalgia.

Then one quiet Thursday evening, a message popped up.

Rhea: Let's plan a trip. Like seriously. No jokes this time.

"Seen."

"Seen."

Ignored.

The familiar blue ticks felt colder than usual. Maybe everyone was just too caught up in the nine-to-whenever rhythm of adulthood. Or maybe no one believed anyone meant anything anymore.

But two hours later:

Ishaan: I'm in. Life's been hell. I need this.

Karan: Only if there are mountains. And Maggi. Non-negotiable.

Aman: You guys say this every 6 months. And it never happens.

Rhea: That's why it should happen now. Before we become those people who only dream out loud, but never move.

Silence followed. But it wasn't the dead kind.

It felt... loaded. Like something was shifting.

Then:

Aman: Okay. Prove me wrong.

That was it. No drumroll. No swelling music.

Just a flicker of warmth — a moment of alignment, fragile but real.

Somewhere between their unwashed coffee mugs and half-done to-do lists, four adults found themselves transported back to who they once were — and who, maybe, they still wanted to be.

1.2 — The Call That Started It All

Later that night, Rhea called Ishaan.

He picked up after three rings. "Didn't expect a call. Everything okay?"

"I'm serious, you know," she said, curled up in bed, the edge of her blanket gripped tight in one hand. "I feel like we're losing something."

"What?"

"Ourselves. Each other. I miss being us."

He let that sit for a second. There was the soft hiss of him lighting a cigarette on the other end. "Yeah. Me too."

Outside her window, the city buzzed faintly — distant traffic, some neighbor's TV echoing a laugh track. But inside, it was just her and the voice of someone who had once felt like home.

"I don't want this to be another idea we kill with excuses," she added, softer now. "Let's make it count."

Ishaan exhaled slowly. "Then we will. Let's escape, Ree. Even if it's just for a while."

The next morning, a new document appeared in the group drive:

Escape Plan ✈?

Color-coded tabs. Suggested dates. Budget estimates.

A spark was officially lit.

1.3 — Choosing the Destination

Over the next few days, the group call became routine.

Each night, someone would pitch a new destination with Google images and hashtags.

Manali? Too commercial.

Jibhi? "We'll be surrounded by Instagrammers with DSLRs and ring lights."

Goa? "What are we, engineering freshers?"

Eventually, Ishaan mentioned something he'd bookmarked years ago. A faded travel blog with grainy pictures but vivid words.

"Deoria Taal," he said. "It's near Chopta. Remote. Untouched. No fancy cafes. No signal. Just a lake. And silence."

Silence on the call.

Then Rhea whispered, "It sounds... perfect."

Karan muttered, "It also sounds freezing. And dangerous."

"Which is exactly why it's perfect," Aman said, for once without sarcasm.

Ishaan smiled to himself. That was the moment it became real.

1.4 — The Logistics War

Choosing the place was easy.

Getting there? That was war.

Coordinating time off was like defusing a bomb.

Rhea had to charm her way through a toxic manager who considered leave requests a personal insult.

Ishaan negotiated with art clients who didn't believe in deadlines unless they were yesterday.

Karan had to finish editing food vlog footage he'd shot months ago — mostly videos of samosas and him yelling "mmm!" dramatically.

Aman, the most structured of them all, faked a client workshop in Lucknow and timed it down to GPS screenshots.

The planning turned them into high-functioning chaos monkeys.

Spreadsheets. Voice notes. Screenshots of trek checklists.

They booked a Zoomcar, stalked Amazon sales for tents, and borrowed half their gear from cousins who had once "almost" trekked Kedarnath.

Late at night, they shared reels of Himalayan sunsets and bear warnings.

They laughed too much. Argued over the playlist.

And slowly, something shifted — not just in the trip, but in them.

It didn't just feel real.

It felt needed.

1.5 — Unspoken Excitements, Unsaid Fears

They never really said why this trip mattered so much.

But reasons hung around the edges, like shadows at dusk.

For Rhea, it was an escape from a job that drained her and a relationship that had become a distant echo.

She hadn't told anyone yet, but she'd drafted the breakup message three times. It sat unsent in her Notes app.

For Ishaan, whose art had lately felt hollow, it was a reset. His sketchbook had been untouched for weeks, and the colors in his mind felt muted.

Karan was all jokes and memes, but beneath it simmered a restlessness — the kind that kept you scrolling at 3 a.m., wondering what exactly you were searching for.

Aman, who lived by slides, stats, and schedules, needed to remember what feeling alive meant — without a calendar invite telling him how.

They didn't put any of this in the group chat.

But it was there.

In the extra emoji Rhea used.

In the way Ishaan started replying quicker.

In how Karan kept sending mountain memes.

And how Aman, for once, didn't say no.

1.6 — The Night Before

On the eve of departure, the group chat buzzed like it hadn't in years.

Karan: Last call for snacks. I have chips, biscuits, and guilt.

Rhea: I have trail mix and tissues. For the snacks. Not the guilt.

Aman: Packed meds. In case Karan eats something "experimental" again.

Ishaan: Sketchbook ready. Let's go.

But offline, the night stretched slower.

Karan rearranged his backpack three times, carefully sliding in his Bluetooth speaker. He cued up a playlist titled Mountains & Madness.

Rhea stared at her jacket — the one that still faintly smelled like someone who used to mean everything. She almost didn't pack it. But did.

Ishaan packed last. He sat on his floor for a long time, staring at a blank canvas leaning against the wall.

Then he tucked a charcoal pencil between the pages of his sketchbook. A quiet promise to himself.

Aman laid out his trekking shoes, laces tied, polished. Then he opened a drawer and found an old photo of the four of them at graduation. He kept it in his wallet.

None of them really slept.

Not because they were anxious.

Because they were ready.

1.7 — Departure Day

5:30 AM.

The world was still half-asleep when they met at the Zoomcar parking lot.

There was no slow-motion hug. No dramatic music.

Just foggy breath, mismatched backpacks, and warm paper cups of chai.

Karan yawned theatrically. "Someone forgot the snacks. I can feel it in my stomach."

Rhea grinned. "Check your bag. You're the snack."

Aman adjusted the rearview mirror. "Drive safe. No selfies while steering. No Bluetooth fights."

"I'm driving," Rhea announced, slipping into the seat like she'd done it a thousand times.

"God help us all," Ishaan muttered, but he was smiling.

The bags were shoved in. The aux was claimed. The playlist crackled to life.

And then — they were off.

Out of the city. Into the haze.

Past the billboards and traffic snarls and the life they were momentarily leaving behind.

None of them knew what lay ahead — just a lake, a promise, and something transcendent waiting in the silence of the hills.

But in that moment, they weren't just friends on a trip.

They were themselves.

And that was everything.

2

The Road Unwinds

"Some roads don't take you away — they bring you back to who you were before the world happened to you."

2.1 — Wheels in Motion

The car rolled out of Delhi just before 6 AM, slicing through the pale early light. A fragile silence lay over the city streets, disturbed only by the occasional honk or rumble of a distant truck.

Sleep still clung stubbornly to their faces — a residue of late nights and busy lives — but the air inside the car was crisp with something else: a tangible, electric sense of freedom, of possibility. The kind that tickles the skin and loosens the chest.

Rhea sat behind the wheel, her sunglasses perched defiantly, even though the sun hadn't quite risen. The dark lenses gave her a quiet armor, a shield against the world still waking around them. Her hands gripped the steering wheel with an unfamiliar mix of excitement and nerves — this was no ordinary drive home from work.

Beside her, Karan rode shotgun, his fingers scrolling rapidly through an endless list of songs on his phone. He argued with the Bluetooth system like an exasperated DJ battling a malfunctioning soundboard, tapping the screen, sighing, and occasionally throwing a grin at Rhea.

In the back seat, Ishaan and Aman had succumbed to the gentle lull of motion, necks bent awkwardly against the headrests, eyes closed but minds still spinning with anticipation. Sometimes Ishaan's fingers twitched as if composing invisible sketches in the air, while Aman's brow furrowed slightly, perhaps rehearsing a presentation he would never give.

Delhi faded behind them — the blaring horns, the tangled crowds, the endless concrete and glass — all dissolving into a blur. Buildings gave way to highways lined with ancient trees, their branches reaching out like whispers from the past. Then came the hills, rising shyly in the distance, shadows softening the edges of the world.

2.2 — Conversations and Curves

By the time they reached Meerut, the car was no longer just a vehicle — it was a capsule of memories, laughter, and confessions.

Karan's voice cut through the low hum of the engine. "Remember when I tried to climb the library gate to impress that girl?"

Rhea chuckled, eyes glinting behind her glasses. "You mean when you almost broke your arm? Yeah, how could I forget?"

"I did impress her," Karan said, puffing out his chest as if reliving the moment. "She still follows me on Instagram."

"That's because you send her memes at 2 AM," Aman muttered, taking a sip of his steaming coffee from the travel mug.

Laughter bubbled up between them, not forced or rehearsed, but the kind that seeps from shared history — from the countless stolen moments, the whispered secrets in dorm rooms, the chaotic nights before exams.

The road curved beneath them like a serpent, winding its way through fields painted gold by the morning sun. Trees leaned inward, casting dappled shadows on the asphalt. Birds flitted past in sudden, frantic bursts, their calls sharp against the engine's steady drone.

Each bend seemed to unspool a thread from their past — the pranks, the heartbreaks, the small victories and devastating losses that had shaped them but somehow never defined them entirely.

2.3 — Pit Stops and Perspectives

By noon, they pulled off at a highway dhaba near Haridwar — a weathered roadside eatery that smelled of frying spices and fresh chai, a haven for weary travelers.

The air was thick with the scent of ghee and cardamom, blending with the dust kicked up by passing trucks. Rhea and Ishaan settled at a wooden table, its surface scarred and sticky, watching pilgrims pass by carrying saffron flags and folded hands pressed to their chests.

"You ever wonder where we'd be if we hadn't met?" Rhea asked softly, voice nearly lost beneath the hum of conversation and clatter of plates.

Ishaan shrugged, a small smile touching his lips. "I'd still be painting strangers and calling it art. Maybe less happy, definitely less grounded."

Rhea smiled back, eyes thoughtful. "You'd still be the most misunderstood genius I know."

At another table, Aman and Karan bickered good-naturedly with the dhaba's cashier over the bill — a playful tradition dating back years, each trying to convince the other that he should pay.

The moment was a pause in their frantic lives — a stillness filled with warmth and quiet joy.

2.4 — Into the Hills

The road beyond Rishikesh was a different world.

The highway narrowed, winding upward through dense forests where towering pines stretched like ancient sentinels. The scent of damp earth and pine needles filled the air, mingling with the faint tang of smoke from distant wood fires.

Traffic thinned to a trickle — just the occasional jeep rumbling past, kicking up clouds of dust that settled like whispers on the trees.

Karan took over driving, the afternoon sun filtering through the canopy and casting flickering light patterns across his face. His playlist shifted to old indie Hindi songs — Prateek Kuhad, Lucky Ali, Mohit Chauhan — the perfect soundtrack for the slow unfolding of the hills.

Ishaan pressed his camera against the window, trying to capture the way sunlight danced like fireflies on the waving branches. He pointed to a family of monkeys perched on a moss-covered rock, chattering and leaping with carefree abandon.

Aman pulled out a worn notebook, fingers tracing the handwritten list of campsites, nearby villages, and emergency contacts. He muttered dates and distances under his breath, a planner even on vacation.

"Do you ever stop planning?" Karan teased.

"Do you ever start?" Aman shot back with a smirk.

Their differences were stark, but somehow they balanced one another, like the jagged peaks and the gentle valleys.

2.5 — Storms and Stillness

As the group neared Devprayag, the sky suddenly darkened, and a swift gust of wind rattled the car's windows.

Raindrops splattered across the windshield, blurring the road ahead. Visibility dropped. Rhea's hands tightened on the grab handle as Karan slowed the car, muscles tense.

"Should we stop?" Aman asked, voice low.

"No. Let's keep going," Karan said through clenched teeth. "It'll pass."

The storm raged for twenty minutes — rain pelting the roof, rivers swelling nearby, the scent of wet pine sharp and alive.

When it finally eased to a drizzle, the mountains around them shimmered — wet, clean, and impossibly green. They pulled over at a viewpoint.

Below, the Bhagirathi and Alaknanda rivers converged in a swirling embrace, muddy and powerful.

Silence fell like a prayer.

"No matter how distant their beginnings," Rhea Murmured, "they are destined to unite as one."

No one replied, but none were silent.

2.6 — Ukhimath at Dusk

They arrived at Ukhimath just as the last light bled from the sky.

The small town was a cluster of stone houses and winding alleys, nestled deep in the Garhwal hills, bathed in a golden dusk haze.

Their homestay was simple but welcoming — run by an elderly couple whose hands were rough from years of work but whose smiles were soft and genuine.

Ginger tea was poured in chipped cups, its warmth seeping into their chilled fingers.

Dinner was served by the hearth — aloo-gobhi, steaming dal, hot rotis that melted on the tongue. The kind of food that tastes like belonging, like history.

Ishaan sat cross-legged on the floor, sketching the homestay dog as it snoozed by the fire. Karan tried (and failed) to flirt with the owner's granddaughter, who simply rolled her eyes and turned away.

Rhea captured a time-lapse of the valley's fading light, her fingers trembling slightly.

Aman sat quietly, his gaze lost in the stars beyond the window, the cold air crisp and biting.

That night, they shared one room — the thin walls barely muffling their whispered laughter and confessions.

The cold pressed in, but it brought them closer — in body and spirit.

2.7 — A Night of Realizations

Long after the others drifted into sleep, Rhea and Ishaan lay awake.

"You ever feel like we're all just pretending to be okay?" Rhea's voice was soft, almost swallowed by the dark.

"All the time," Ishaan admitted. "But sometimes pretending is better than falling apart."

Rhea turned toward the window, watching the faint silhouette of the hills against the night sky. "I don't want this trip to end."

"It's only just started," he whispered.

"She just smiled faintly, then headed back to call it a night."

They fell asleep not because exhaustion claimed them — but because the mountains had wrapped them in a fragile kind of safety.

2.8 — The Final Drive

Dawn broke cold and pale.

They packed quickly, the excitement in their movements barely contained.

Mist clung to the air, curling around terraced fields and scattered stone homes.

Villagers greeted them with quiet nods, the simple acts of daily life unfolding unhurried.

The car wound steadily toward Sari village — the base of their trek.

As they parked and stretched, the path ahead beckoned — a steep trail carved through forests and meadows, promises etched in every step.

They weren't running away anymore.

They were coming home.

3

Into The Stillness

"It's not the miles that make some paths longer, but the growth they quietly demand before you can walk them."

3.1 — A Late Start

Despite noble intentions and repeated alarms, the group didn't leave Sari village until around 3:30 PM. The sun hung lazily above the hills, already starting its slow descent. The sky had that golden hue only found in mountain regions—soft, warm, almost nostalgic. It painted the rooftops of Sari in honeyed light, casting long shadows on cobbled paths lined with stone huts and prayer flags swaying gently in the breeze.

Rhea stood at the start of the trail, scanning the route with a mixture of anxiety and excitement. Her backpack, secured tightly against her shoulders, tugged at her spine, but she didn't care. The cold had a bite now, crisp enough to sting the nostrils when inhaled too fast. She wrapped her scarf tighter, adjusted her beanie, and turned toward the group.

Aman double-checked the time on his watch. "We were supposed to start by noon. Noon. This is how horror stories begin."

"Please," Karan huffed, stuffing trail mix into his mouth. "The trek is two kilometers. That's like walking to the corner store. Don't get dramatic."

Ishaan, ever the quiet observer, was fiddling with the settings on his DSLR. He glanced over his lens and smirked. "You climbed three stairs this morning and needed Gatorade."

"Details, Ishaan. Don't get bogged down by details."

Rhea rolled her eyes but smiled. "Can we not waste more time? It gets dark quickly here."

With that, they began.

The trail started off gently, winding past the last few houses of the village. Stone steps led upwards, flanked by wheat fields on one side and thickening clusters of trees on the other. A few curious villagers, wrapped in layers, watched them with quiet amusement as the group passed. A little girl waved from a porch. Rhea waved back.

There was something grounding about those first few minutes. The hum of city life was gone, replaced by the crunch of boots on gravel, the occasional chirp of a bird, and the soft whisper of pine needles brushing the breeze. The lake felt like a distant promise. Right now, the journey was everything.

3.2 — The Trail Tightens

Half an hour in, the cheerful chatter began to fade as the trail steepened.

The canopy of pine trees thickened around them. The air turned cooler, cleaner. It carried a scent of earth, resin, and something older—something timeless. It felt like walking into a sacred space. Sunlight slanted through the branches in fractured shards, catching on dust motes and moss. The forest seemed to breathe.

Karan trailed at the back now, one hand gripping the side of his thigh as he panted. "Guys, I swear this trek wasn't in the brochure."

Rhea, a few feet ahead, glanced over her shoulder. "You didn't read any brochure."

"Still. Someone should've warned me."

"You were warned," Aman called out, slightly winded but managing a steady pace. "In that ten-slide itinerary I sent. Which you reacted to with a poop emoji."

Karan gasped dramatically. "Sarcasm under duress is a war crime."

Ishaan chuckled but didn't stop walking. His camera swung from his neck as he occasionally paused to click photos—fallen pinecones, birds mid-flight, and once, a tree trunk carved with initials from another time.

Despite the banter, all of them were slowly falling under the spell of the place. There was something hypnotic about the rhythm of the forest—the soft thud of boots on earth, the crackle of dry leaves, the rhythmic rise and fall of their breath.

None of them admitted it, but they all felt it.

That invisible presence.

The quiet.

The deep, ancient kind of quiet that didn't feel empty—it felt full. As if the forest knew things. As if it had seen hundreds of people pass through, carrying laughter and heartbreak and hope, only to leave lighter than they came.

Somewhere, a branch snapped. A bird took flight with a startled cry. They paused for a second, eyes scanning the trees.

"Just a monkey," Ishaan said after a beat.

"Or a yeti," Karan muttered. "If I go missing, please make a good movie about me."

Rhea smiled to herself, but her fingers unconsciously tightened around the strap of her backpack.

3.3 — Shadows Lengthen

By 5 PM, the sky was no longer gold—it was ochre, deepening into amber. The trail had grown thinner, the air colder. The trees had pressed in tighter, the undergrowth denser, the silence more pronounced.

They reached a fork in the path, where a carved wooden sign pointed left:

Deoria Taal — 700 m

Ishaan paused, one hand on the weather-worn post. He looked around.

"Do you guys feel... I don't know. Like we're being watched?"

Rhea turned to him, the light catching in her eyes. "What do you mean?"

He shrugged, suddenly unsure. "Not in a creepy way. Just... like we're not alone."

Aman exhaled, fog misting in front of his face. "There are probably animals nearby. Leopards, maybe. Or langurs. Nothing weird."

Karan gulped audibly. "Why would you say 'leopards' so casually? Why not butterflies?"

"Because butterflies don't stalk you at dusk."

The trail curved sharply now, bordered by dense pine groves on one side and a sheer drop on the other. The temperature had dropped noticeably. Every breath was visible. The path was covered in scattered needles and patches of frost.

"They slowed down—not out of fear, but out of caution."

The mountain had changed. What was earlier a friendly welcome was now a quiet warning.

Move with care. You are not in charge here.

The hush was thick now. Every footstep felt louder than it should. Even the wind seemed to have grown shy, whispering instead of howling.

They didn't speak for a while. Words felt intrusive.

3.4 — Arrival at Dusk

At around 6:30 PM, just as the light began to fail, the forest gave way to a sudden clearing.

It felt like stepping into another world.

Deoria Taal stretched out in front of them—serene, glassy, untouched. The lake caught the last hues of the sunset, reflecting them in gentle ripples. It looked like someone had poured starlight into a basin and forgotten to stir.

In the distance, the snowy outline of Chaukhamba peak loomed silently, bathed in the softest shades of violet and rose gold. Not a single sound broke the stillness—no crickets, no breeze. Just the occasional echo of their breath.

But what held their gaze wasn't just the lake.

It was a tent.

Small. Grey. Perfectly pitched under a crooked pine on the far side of the lake, just beyond the water's edge.

There were no other campers. No second tent. No firewood stacks. No murmurs or music or flickering lights.

Just that tent. And silence.

"Someone's here," Rhea said, breaking the hush.

They stood still, the weight of the moment settling in.

Ishaan raised his camera instinctively, then lowered it. "That wasn't on the plan."

Aman scanned the perimeter. "Well... technically, it's a public campsite. People come solo all the time."

"Yeah, but do they camp without a fire? Or any light?" Karan asked. "Maybe it's a monk."

"Or a serial killer," Karan added helpfully.

Rhea ignored him. "We should still pitch our tents. Maybe over there." She pointed to a flat patch about twenty meters away, nestled near a ring of stones that looked like an old firepit.

They began unpacking in silence. Even Karan didn't joke anymore.

Something about the lake demanded reverence.

4

The Encounter

The lake shimmered in silver silence.

A lone tent stood by the water, its soft light flickering like a story waiting to be told. And beside it, a girl sat — calm, still, as if she belonged to the lake.

She looked about their age — draped in a dark olive jacket, hair pulled into a messy braid. She was calmly brewing something in a small kettle.

She looked up at them with curious, unstartled eyes.

The four friends stopped in their tracks.

"Okay, I did *not* expect this," Karan whispered. "Is she... real?"

Rhea took the lead. "Hi!" she called out.

The girl looked up, smiled. "Hey. You guys made it just before the cold gets mean."

Her voice radiated warmth — like chai on a winter morning.

"We weren't expecting anyone else here," Aman said.

"Neither was I," she replied. "But there's enough sky for all of us."

Tents were pitched, jackets zipped, and soon, a small fire danced in the center. The woods crackled quietly around

21

them, and the lake watched in perfect silence.

Rhea unpacked their dinner supplies — instant noodles, boiled eggs, and some paneer rolls wrapped in foil. "It's not fancy," she said, "but it's hot."

"Smells amazing," the girl said, accepting a plate.

"I'm Rhea. This is Aman, our forever planner. Karan — don't take him seriously. And Ishaan — our walking playlist and poet."

"With a gentle smile, the girl looked at each of them. 'Aanya,' she said, introducing herself to the group."

They ate by the fire, legs stretched out on camping mats, steam rising into the night. Laughter echoed through the pines as stories poured out — near-missed exams, failed love stories, college pranks.

Aanya listened more than she spoke, but when she did, her words were measured — like she chose them carefully, each carrying a memory.

"You've been here before?" Ishaan asked, passing her another roll.

She nodded. "Once. A long time ago. With someone I loved."

Silence.

Aman, trying to keep things light, asked, "You guys used to come often?"

"Only once," Aanya said, her gaze on the lake. "We planned many trips. But life... didn't keep up with us."

There was something in the way she said it — not bitter, not broken. Just... unfinished.

Karan, unusually quiet, glanced at her. "Did he...?"

She looked at him. Then down at her food.

"He left without saying goodbye."

The fire cracked. Somewhere in the trees, an owl hooted.

Rhea gently changed the subject. "Do you always travel alone?"

Aanya smiled. "Not always. But solitude... it teaches you to hear what people don't say."

That line hit Ishaan hardest. He scribbled it into his notebook without even realizing.

After dinner, Aman passed around coffee. Aanya held hers and took a sip after inhaling it's aroma. "I love the smell," she said. "It always reminded me of him."

She stared at the steam curling into the cold air. "To me, coffee by the lake taste's like love."

The group fell silent again.

Finally, she stood. "Thank you. For the food. And the warmth. I'll head to sleep."

"Goodnight, Aanya," Rhea said, gently.

Aanya smiled one last time. "Goodnight. See you in the morning."

She stepped into her tent, zipped it shut.

And that was that.

Later, as they cleaned up and zipped into their own tents, Aman murmured, "There's something about her."

"She's grieving," Rhea said softly. "But she's not stuck. She's... floating."

"She feels like poetry," Ishaan added.

"Yeah," Karan said, gazing at the tent. "Like something beautiful that already ended, but you're still lucky you saw it once."

"Damn Karan, who knew a tiny brain of yours could think something this deep?" Aman said it, clearly surprised but with a mocking grin.

Rhea and Ishaan burst into laughter, while Karan made face's and tossed a few playful profanities into the mix, lightening the mood that had been tense, just moment's earlier during the conversation about 'Aanya.'

"Their banter carried on late into the night, until they drifted off to sleep beneath a moon that felt almost too quiet, too serene."

5

The Disappearance

"Some goodbyes dissolve into silence, vanishing like the mist with the rise of the sun."

5.1 — The Empty Morning

The first light crept over Deoria Taal like a secret — soft, pale, and tentative. Mist lingered on the water's surface, and dew coated every blade of grass in a fragile silver sheen. It was the kind of morning that felt untouched, like the world had held its breath all night and was only now starting to exhale.

Rhea stirred first. Her eyes fluttered open to the cool kiss of the mountain air seeping through the thin tent fabric. She reached for her phone to check the time — 6:12 AM. Slipping out of her sleeping bag, she unzipped the tent flap quietly, not wanting to wake the others.

The lake greeted her in full stillness. The mist swirled over the water like slow breath. For a long moment, she just stood there, soaking in the view. Then she stretched her arms wide and called, softly but cheerfully, "Guys... wake up. It's beautiful out."

One by one, the others emerged — Aman, rubbing his neck; Karan, yawning exaggeratedly; and Ishaan, groggy but camera-ready.

"Damn," Karan muttered, stepping out. "This is... insanely peaceful."

But Aman wasn't looking at the lake. His eyes were scanning the far end of the clearing — where Aanya's tent had stood.

His brow furrowed. He walked a few steps forward. Then a few more.

And stopped.

He turned back toward the group. "Guys. Her tent... it's gone."

5.2 — Gone Without a Trace

"What do you mean gone?" Rhea asked, frowning.

Aman pointed. "Right there. That's where she was last night, remember?"

The four of them walked to the spot together. The earth was undisturbed. No flattened grass. No ash from a fire. No food wrappers, no tarp impressions. Not even footprints. It was like she had never been there.

"No way," Karan whispered. "This is some prank, right?"

"She left in the middle of the night?" Rhea asked, glancing at the trail. "But we were just twenty feet away. We'd have heard her."

"She was alone," Aman added. "Packing a tent takes time. It's noisy."

Ishaan crouched down near the boulder they had all sat around the previous night. On top of it sat her coffee cup. Still full. Steamless now, but untouched — like it had been preserved in time.

He reached out but didn't touch it. "This... this doesn't feel normal."

The birds chirped distantly. A faint breeze whispered through the trees. But for the group, it felt like the world had gone eerily quiet.

Aman turned and looked out toward the lake. "I don't get it. She was here. We all saw her. We spoke with her."

"She told us about the guy she used to come here with," Rhea said. "How they had planned trips they never took..."

"Maybe this was her goodbye," Ishaan murmured.

"Don't say it like that," Karan snapped. "Like she's... not real."

But no one replied.

5.3 — Traces in the Mist

They split up and searched the area — half out of instinct, half from an aching disbelief that someone could vanish so completely. Rhea walked the lake's perimeter, scanning for even a thread of cloth or stray footprint. Aman climbed a short ridge to get a better view. Karan stayed near the tents, nervously pacing, while Ishaan sat on the boulder and scribbled distractedly into his notebook.

Nothing.

No footprints. No voices. No other campers. No path she could've taken unnoticed.

Karan finally broke the silence. "I'm officially creeped out. Like... horror-movie-level creeped out."

Rhea returned, shaking her head. "Nothing. Not even a crushed leaf."

"She was here," Aman repeated, this time more to himself. "I'm not going crazy. She spoke to us."

"She told me something," Ishaan said, still staring at the untouched cup. "That solitude teaches you to hear what people don't say. It didn't feel like a casual thought."

"Do you think she planned to vanish?" Rhea asked.

Karan scoffed, though it lacked real conviction. "People don't just disappear like that."

But again — no one said a word more.

Because deep down, they all felt it: something was off. Something was... wrong.

5.4 — Descent into Uncertainty

Packing up took longer than expected. Not because they had too much gear — but because they kept pausing. Looking back. Double-checking. Listening for a rustle that never came.

Even as they zipped up their bags and folded the tents, the sense of Aanya lingered like a perfume — subtle, but present. In the grass. In the air. In their minds.

As they began to descent down the same trail they'd climbed the previous evening, a fog rolled in over the upper forest. The sun was climbing, but the mist clung low and thick, muting the colors and sound.

They barely spoke on the way down. Occasionally, one of them would begin to say something — a memory from last night, a comment about her — but stop halfway. As if naming it made it less believable.

They paused for water near a bend in the trail.

Karan sat down on a rock. "Okay, let's just put this out there. Do any of you think... she was real?"

"Of course she was real," Aman snapped. "She had a name. A voice.."

Rhea sat next to him, arms folded. "I think... she was real. But not entirely of this world. Like something stuck in between."

"She felt like poetry," Ishaan murmured. "Like the kind of person who doesn't just live in the world... but passes through it."

No one disagreed.

5.5 — The Dhaba

Halfway down, they stopped at a small **dhaba** — just a wooden shack with two benches and the smell of fresh parathas.

The owner, an middle aged man with deep lines on his face, greeted them warmly. "Aa gaye upar se? Sahi waqt pe aa gaye. Baarish hone wali hai."

The tea came, but none of them touched it.

"She was different, wasn't she?" Rhea finally said.

Aman nodded. "Strange, yeah... but comforting."

"She said something," Ishaan murmured, as if thinking out loud. "While holding her coffee last night. 'Coffee by the lake tastes like love.'"

The dhaba owner, overhearing, froze mid-pour.

He turned, eyes narrowing. "What did you just say?"

"Uh... she said coffee by the lake tastes like love. Why?"

The dhaba owner sat down slowly, his hands trembling. His voice dropped to a whisper.

"That's what *she* used to say. My Aanya."

The name hit them like cold wind.

"She said it every time we camped," he continued. "That was her line, her belief. No one else could've known."

6

A Promise Unkept

The steam from the chai rose slowly, spiraling into the still morning air. The dhaba was quiet now. A fly buzzed somewhere near the window, and the only sound was the occasional creak of the fan above. The four friends sat around the table, their earlier laughter now silenced by the weight of something unseen, something heavy and cold that had taken a seat beside them.

Raghav the dhaba owner — sat across from them his weathered face unreadable at first. But when Ishaan, still pale from the shock, slid the sketch of the girl across the table, something in Raghav's eyes trembled. His fingers hovered over the paper for a moment before he gently picked it up.

His thumb lightly brushed over the charcoal lines.

"Where did you meet her?" he asked, voice rough like gravel.

"At Deoria Taal," Karan answered quietly. "Last night. She was camping alone. Said we could set up near her."

"We made her coffee," added Rhea, her voice distant. "She said… 'coffee by the lake tastes like love.'"

Raghav closed his eyes.

Silence.

Then he opened them again — and they were full of grief.

"That was my Aanya," he said.

The name lingered in the air like incense.

"She died ten years ago today."

The friends sat frozen, each feeling a chill rise up their spine.

Aman tried to speak, but no words came.

"She used to say that line," Raghav continued, eyes fixed on the sketch. "'Coffee by the lake tastes like love.' whenever we went camping. She said the lake made her feel alive. Peaceful."

He took a slow breath.

"We were engaged. College sweethearts. She was the kind of girl who left bits of poetry in the margins of her textbooks, who believed in signs from the universe and the healing power of rain. She loved wildflowers. And quiet places."

His voice cracked slightly.

"She dreamed of coming to Uttarakhand and starting a café by the hills. A tiny wooden place, by the lake, where people could talk, write, dream."

The friends leaned in — Aanya was no longer a mystery, but a memory taking form in front of them.

"We came here ten years ago," Raghav continued. "Just like you. A short trip. No plans. Just her and me and the stars. We trekked to the lake late — just like you did — and set up our tent in the dark."

His hands curled slowly on the table.

"She was tired. I told her to rest. I went into the woods to gather firewood... but I was gone too long."

The air seemed to still as he paused.

"When I returned, she wasn't there."

No one breathed.

"I searched. For hours. Calling her name. The forest felt different. Off. I finally found her… not far, but far enough. She had slipped on the slope behind the lake. She'd fallen onto rocks. Her leg was broken. Her skull was bleeding. There was blood allover. She was shivering."

Raghav's voice began to shake.

"She smiled at me through the pain. And said, 'Don't cry. Just stay with me. I'll be okay.'"

He looked away.

"But she wasn't. The help came too late. She died in my arms."

Rhea pressed her fingers against her lips, tears slipping down her cheeks.

"She said she'd be back. She said she'd always be there… waiting."

Raghav looked out the window as if searching for her silhouette among the trees.

"I couldn't leave. I never did. I built this place here, hoping she'd come back. Not as a ghost… just as a feeling. And some nights, she does."

He looked at each of them, one by one.

"Did she say her name?"

The group nodded in agreement.

"That was all she shared, nothing beyond her name." Karan replied.

"She never does," Raghav whispered.

They sat in silence for a long time.

"Why us?" Aman asked finally. "Why did she appear to *us*?"

"Maybe she saw something in you," Raghav said. "Something she recognized. Something pure. Or maybe…

maybe you reminded her of the life we never had."

Ishaan slid the sketch back toward himself. "She looked so real. So alive."

"She is," Raghav said softly. "In some way, she is."

Rhea reached for her diary, flipping back to something she had jotted the night before.

"She said something else," she murmured. "'I loved someone who wasn't afraid of silence. He knew how to listen without needing to speak.'"

Raghav smiled faintly — a mix of pain and pride.

"That was me."

Outside, a soft breeze passed through the trees.

The group stepped out of the dhaba, and Raghav walked them to the edge of the clearing. The lake wasn't visible from here, but they could feel its presence — quiet, distant, waiting.

"Every year, on this day," Raghav said, "she finds her way back. Sometimes in whispers. Sometimes in dreams. Sometimes... more."

He looked toward the hills.

"Maybe she needed to be seen. To be remembered."

Aanya's scarf — the one she had worn last night — was now hanging gently from a tree branch nearby.

No one said a word.

Raghav walked over and gently took it down, holding it to his chest.

"She always loved the wind," he murmured.

7

Echoes In The Hills

The road twisted behind them like a memory refusing to let go.

Their SUV rolled slowly through the winding hills, trees casting long, slanted shadows across the path as afternoon gave way to dusk. Normally, they would've been bantering, making fun of each other's playlists, or arguing over which café to stop at next. But today, the car was wrapped in silence — the kind of silence that comes when you've seen something your heart can't explain.

Rhea sat by the window, head leaning on the glass. The light danced on her face, but her eyes didn't move — she was lost in thought, replaying every word Aanya had said. Her warmth. Her poise. Her sorrow.

Ishaan sat with his sketchbook closed in his lap. The drawing of Aanya — the one he'd made after that brief night — rested inside it, though he hadn't dared to look at it since morning. Something about it unnerved him now. Not because it was wrong... but because it felt more *right* than it should have. He had drawn her from memory. But now it felt like she had drawn herself through his hand.

Karan kept his eyes on the road. One hand on the wheel, one hanging loosely out of the window. Every few minutes, he'd glance into the rearview mirror — as if expecting her reflection to appear in the back seat, smiling that soft, poetic smile.

Aman finally spoke, his voice quieter than usual.

"Do you guys think... we were supposed to meet her?"

No one answered for a moment. The question didn't need an immediate reply.

Rhea finally said, "No one else was there. Not a single other tent. And she said yes to us without hesitation... like she was waiting."

"She was waiting," Ishaan muttered. "For *him*. For Raghav."

"But then why show up to us?" Karan asked. "Why now? Ten years later?"

No one could answer.

The silence stretched.

They stopped for fuel at a small, run-down petrol pump. The station attendant had headphones on, lost in some Garhwali folk song, barely noticing them. The air here felt colder than it should have.

As Aman stretched his legs, he noticed something strange — a worn-out poster stapled to the wooden side of the small shop. It was old, the edges curled and faded by sun and rain. But what caught his eye was the sketch.

It was a drawing of a woman — smiling, standing near a lake, wind in her hair.

Aanya.

He froze.

"Karan!" he called out. The others rushed over.

"It's her," Ishaan whispered. "That's my sketch. But... I never showed it to anyone."

At the bottom of the poster, almost hidden under layers of tape, was a message in handwritten blue ink:

"In memory of Aanya Verma. The lake remembers."

That night, they stayed at a small guesthouse near Ukhimath. The caretaker was a quiet old man who barely spoke but kept the tea flowing and the rooms clean. After dinner, they all sat in one room, cross-legged on the floor, lit by a single yellow lamp.

Ishaan finally opened the sketchbook.

The drawing was... different.

The lines were the same. But now, the expression in Aanya's eyes seemed changed. Not fearful. Not mournful.

Pleading.

"She's not done," Rhea said softly.

Everyone looked at her.

"I don't know how I know. I just... feel it. That she didn't come back to haunt us. She came to *ask* something."

"What though?" Aman asked. "Closure?"

"No," Karan said slowly. "A message. For Raghav. Or maybe... for herself."

There was a moment of pause before he added, "We need to go back."

The next morning, they packed light — just enough for one more night under the stars. The trek up felt heavier this time, not physically, but emotionally. The trees didn't seem menacing — they felt like silent watchers, guardians of a secret the world had forgotten.

By the time they reached Deoria Taal, it was just past four in the evening.

The lake was exactly as they had left it — serene, reflective, untouched. But something felt... different. The air was crisper. The silence, deeper.

They pitched their tents again. This time, just theirs.

No other tents in sight.

No sign of Aanya.

Yet.

As night fell, they gathered by the fire, making coffee again. Ishaan sat with his sketchbook, redrawing the same image — trying to understand what it wanted to tell him. Rhea walked to the edge of the lake, watching the stars reflect on the water.

Then she saw it.

On the other side of the lake, near a fallen log — a faint figure. Not a shadow. Not a hallucination. Just... a presence.

"Aman," she whispered. "Look."

He joined her. Then Karan. Then Ishaan.

The figure stood there for a second. And then vanished.

"She's here," Ishaan said quietly.

They didn't chase. Didn't panic.

Instead, they sat back by the fire and waited.

An hour passed.

Then another.

The moon rose higher.

And then... she came.

From behind the same trees, slowly, calmly, she walked toward them. The fire flickered. The wind stirred.

Aanya.

Only Ishaan saw her at first — and this time, he didn't speak.

She sat across from him, looking directly into his eyes.

"Your drawing," she said, her voice almost not real, "shows me what I was. But not who I became."

Ishaan's hands trembled. "Then tell me."

She smiled. "Tell *him*... I wasn't afraid. I just didn't want him to wait forever."

The wind carried her words like a song.

"He stayed," Ishaan said.

"I know," she replied. "But now... he can stop."

A pause. A sadness in her smile.

"Thank you."

And then, like mist rising from the lake, she was gone.

The others didn't see her. But they *felt* it. A shift in the air. A release. The fire calmed. The lake stilled.

"She said goodbye," Ishaan said softly.

As they lay in their tents that night, none of them slept. But none were afraid either. The weight of the unknown had lifted, replaced by something peaceful.

In the silence of the forest, they heard it — not a whisper, not a voice — but a *feeling*.

The hills echo what the heart cannot say.

8
The Unsent Letter

The dhaba was closed that day.

A weathered lock hung from the door latch, creaking in the breeze that swept down from the hills. It was the first time in years that Raghav hadn't opened the shutters at 6 AM sharp. No hot chai. No potatoes sizzling on the iron tawa. Just silence, and the rustling of old trees remembering things the world had forgotten.

He stood at the edge of the clearing, a scarf in his hands. Her scarf — the one the kids said had been hanging by the tree.

It still smelled faintly of lavender and cold mountain air.

The four friends had left that morning — eyes heavy but hearts lightened. Raghav had watched them go from the steps of the dhaba, not saying much, just nodding quietly when they waved.

It wasn't over. Not yet.

And he knew it.

After they were gone, he went back inside. The wooden floor creaked under his weight as he stepped into the small storeroom in the back — a place he hadn't entered in years.

Dust floated in the air like memories suspended in time.

He found her old rucksack tucked beneath a worn woollen shawl. He had kept it all this time. It still had her handwriting on the flap: "Aanya's Wanderbag – Do not open unless you believe in magic."

Raghav smiled sadly.

He opened it.

Inside were things that hadn't aged. A tiny compass. A tin box of instant coffee. A necklace made of pine cones she had once crafted during a silly evening. A crumpled polaroid of both of them — younger, freer, madly in love — smiling with the lake behind them.

And a letter.

Folded twice, its corners yellowed. Addressed in her handwriting.

"To Raghav — in case I forget to say goodbye."

He sat down on the floor, legs crossed like a schoolboy, and unfolded it slowly. His hands trembled.

Aanya's Letter – Ten Years Ago

My dearest Raghav,

If you're reading this, I couldn't tell you in person. Maybe I was too stubborn. Maybe I left too soon. Or maybe the universe played one of its cruel tricks.

I hope you forgive me. Not just for going, but for dreaming too loudly and pulling you into those dreams.

I want you to know — I was never afraid of leaving. I was afraid of leaving you. Of not being there to grow old with you, to see our little café by the lake, to read books under the sun while you argued over tea recipes with tourists.

But if I go, and you're still here...

Please don't freeze your life in my memory. Don't build a home out of grief. I'll always be near — in the wind that ruffles the lake, in the laughter of strangers sipping coffee by your dhaba, in the silence that never quite feels alone.

You don't need to wait for me.

I already found you.

That was enough.

Yours, in every lifetime,

Aanya

P.S. The coffee by the lake really does taste like love. Don't forget to offer it to those who stop by your cafe.

Raghav pressed the letter to his chest, eyes shut, shoulders shaking.

Ten years. Ten long years of waiting, mourning, hoping. And here, in these words — written before she had ever vanished — was permission to live again.

He had built a dhaba for her.

Now maybe, it was time to open a life for himself.

That Evening – Return of the Friends

The four of them sat once again at their favorite table outside the dhaba. The sun was setting behind the hills, turning the sky into a palette of orange, gold, and violet. This time, Raghav sat with them — not as the man haunted by the past, but as someone who had just found something he lost long ago.

He handed Ishaan the letter.

They read it in silence. Rhea's fingers curled into a soft fist. Aman looked away, wiping his eyes discreetly.

"It's beautiful," Ishaan whispered.

"It's her," Raghav said.

There was peace in his voice.

"She came to say goodbye," Karan murmured.

"No," Raghav replied gently. "She came so I could finally say goodbye."

Later that night, Raghav took out his old box of wooden boards. He hadn't painted in years. But something called to him.

He painted a new sign for the dhaba.

"Café Aanya – Where Coffee Tastes Like Love."

The next morning, when travelers stopped by, they were greeted with that new board, and a steaming cup of love by the lake.

And Aanya — she lived in every warm sip, every silent smile, and every whispered promise that some goodbyes are just another way to say, I'll see you again.

9
The Things We Carry Home

A Day Later – On the Way Back to Delhi

The SUV cruised steadily down the mountain roads, now no longer a vehicle of escape, but of quiet return.

The four friends didn't speak much. Words felt smaller than the experience they had shared. The valley fell behind them like a memory — Deoria Taal, the lake, Aanya, Raghav — a story that would stay with them long after the journey ended.

But something inside each of them had shifted. Deeply.

And none of them would return the same.

Rhea – The Weight of Wonder

Rhea scrolled through the photos on her phone, stopping at one she had taken absentmindedly — the lake under moonlight. She had clicked it the night they met Aanya, with no idea that the moment was sacred.

The photo was blurry, slightly overexposed. But right at the edge of the frame was a faint outline.

Maybe just light. Maybe a shadow.

Or maybe something more.

Rhea stared at her phone one last time.

The breakup message she had typed before the trip still sat unsent in her drafts — a quiet testament to the uncertainty she had carried with her. But something had shifted up there, among the still waters and the love story that never found closure. Watching her friends laugh, still shaken yet whole, she realized not all endings had to be written in haste. Some, like the letter that never leaves your hand, were meant to teach you the value of staying — a little longer, a little stronger. With a sigh, she deleted the message. Maybe it wasn't time to let go. Not yet.

She turned the screen off.

Rhea was a rationalist. She didn't believe in ghosts, signs, or omens.

But something about Aanya refused to fit into logic.

That night by the lake had reawakened something she had lost — wonder.

Her job in Delhi was demanding. Structured. She had learned to measure success in hours billed and presentations delivered. But this trip — this encounter — had taught her that some things couldn't be measured.

Like silence shared around a fire.

Or a love that waited across death for closure.

Or the way coffee could carry a memory.

Back in Delhi, Rhea stood at her window with a blank journal in her hand — the one she had bought months ago and never used. She opened the first page and wrote:

"I met a girl who was already gone.

And yet, she showed me the way forward."

She didn't know what kind of life she would build after this — but she knew it would have more stories. More soul. More pause.

Ishaan – The Drawing That Drew Him Back

Ishaan returned home to his small studio apartment — walls lined with art he no longer connected with. Abstract pieces, commercial assignments, branding mockups.

He stood before his easel, staring at a blank canvas for hours.

And then he picked up his charcoal pencil.

He didn't paint Aanya this time.

He painted her absence.

A silhouette sitting by a lake. No face, no figure — just space. Longing. Memory. Presence in emptiness.

It was the most powerful thing he had ever created.

The next morning, he emailed his gallery manager.

"Cancel the exhibit. I'm working on something new."

Karan – A Mirror in the Mountains

Karan had always been the loudest, the messiest, the one who never took anything seriously. Life, to him, had always been a sprint — from joke to joke, party to party, plan to plan.

But for the first time, he had sat with stillness. He had watched someone love without conditions, wait without resentment, and say goodbye without bitterness.

He couldn't stop thinking about what Aanya had said through her letter:

"Don't build a home out of grief."

He realized he had been building something out of fear — avoiding commitment, dodging depth, always keeping things casual.

Two weeks later, he called up Meher — the girl he had dated on and off for years.

This time, he didn't ghost her.

He told her about Aanya.

They sat at a rooftop café as he poured his heart out. She didn't speak — just held his hand across the table.

That night, Karan deleted all his dating apps.

For once, he wasn't looking for a distraction.

He was ready to build something real.

Aman – The One Who Finally Believed

Aman had always been skeptical. Practical. A problem-solver. His world was made of cause and effect, evidence and logic.

But Deoria Taal had made him question everything.

He had seen Aanya disappear. Heard her speak. Watched the lake respond in silence to something unseen.

It hadn't been a horror story.

It had been sacred.

Back in Noida, Aman sat in his study surrounded by trekking gear and journals.

He opened a new notebook and titled the first page:

"A LAKE TO REMEMBER."

He had no idea what he would write.

He only knew this: the mountains were more than rocks. Lakes more than water. People more than bodies.

He had witnessed something the city could never explain.

And he wanted more of it.

A Package Arrives

Two weeks later, a package arrived at Ishaan's address. No name. No return label.

Inside was a small wooden box.

Inside the box — a folded scarf, a tin of coffee beans, and a hand-written note:

To the four of you —

Thank you for listening when no one else could. Thank you for reminding me I was remembered.

You didn't just find me. You helped me leave.

With love,

A.

The handwriting was unmistakably Aanya's.

Café Aanya – A Year Later

A small board hangs outside a wooden café near Ukhimath.

The sign says:

"Café Aanya — Where Coffee Tastes Like Love."

Raghav still makes the best coffee in Uttarakhand. Sometimes, he reads her letter aloud to travelers who stop by.

He tells them a story of a girl by the lake.

And how some love stories don't need an ending — just a place to rest.

That summer, a group of tourists stop by. One of them — a young woman — pauses before entering.

She stares at the photo hanging beside the door: A beautiful girl by the lake, sunlight in her hair and something unreadable in her eyes.

She smiles and whispers, "You were real, weren't you?"

The wind rustles through the trees.

And somewhere, a scarf dances softly in the air.

Some stories aren't written — they are felt first.

This was one of them.

"A Lake to Remember" was never meant to be just a tale of a road trip or a mysterious girl by a lake.

It was about the people we meet for a moment, who somehow stay with us forever.

About the silence between words. About promises made under stars.

And about places, quiet, untouched places, that become keepers of our emotions long after we leave.

If this story stayed with you, even for a little while, then perhaps the lake remembers you too.

Thank you for walking this path with me, one page at a time.

- *[Srinivasan Naidu]*